THE
EMPEROR'S GARDEN

by FERIDA WOLFF

pictures by KATHY OSBORN

TAMBOURINE BOOKS

NEW YORK

Library of Congress Cataloging in Publication Data

Wolff, Ferida, 1946–   The emperor's garden/by Ferida Wolff; illustrated by Kathy Osborn. —1st ed. p. cm.

Summary: The villagers' plan to create a splendid garden for their emperor gets bogged down in jealous arguments, happily

resolved when the emperor himself comes to visit. [1. Gardens—Fiction. 2. Kings, queens, rulers, etc.—Fiction.

3. China—Fiction.] I. Osborn, Kathy, ill. II. Title. PZ7.W82124Em 1994 93-14751 CIP AC

ISBN 0-688-11651-5. — ISBN 0-688-11652-3 (lib. bdg.)

1 3 5 7 9 10 8 6 4 2

First edition

For my dear friend Claire

F.W.

For Andy and Nancy

K.O.

Once there was a simple village beside a river in China. Its people were poor but very agreeable. They laughed when they talked and smiled when they worked. Everyone in the village was a relative or a friend.

Each year after the monsoon season, the Supreme Emperor of All China passed through the village on his way to his summer palace in the north.

The people would stop work for the day to line the main street. There, with bowed heads, they paid respect to the emperor. They always hoped that the emperor would stop in their little village, but they had nothing to offer him and the caravan silently moved on.

One day the schoolteacher had a bold plan.

"Let us do something special for the emperor so that he will stop and honor our poor village," he said.

The villagers were very excited by the idea. They talked about it for days, thinking first of one thing then another, until they all agreed that they would create a garden for the emperor.

"It will be a most splendid garden!" they said.

The villagers decided to put it by the river. Then they started to work at once, for the creation of a splendid garden would take time.

As the villagers worked the schoolteacher wrote a letter in his finest calligraphy, inviting the emperor to visit the garden on his way to the Summer Palace.

The farmer grew a special crop of watermelons and placed the firmest by the riverbank for the emperor's delight.

"We must call this the Garden of Best Harvest," said the farmer, "for these are my best melons."

But for the first time, the gardener disagreed with the farmer.

"Your melons will one day rot," she said. "I have planted this most wonderful peach tree, which will last a long time. Everyone knows that peaches mean long life. We should call this the Garden of Long Life."

"Do not forget about my virtuous pond," argued the ditchdigger, who rarely argued about anything. "It is evenly cut and nicely rounded. Should we not call this the Round Pond Garden?"

"No," called out the children. "We have picked five hundred of the smoothest stones to place on the bottom of the pond. Let us name this the Five-Hundred-Stone Garden."

"But what is the value of a pond if there is nothing but dull-colored stones to look upon?" asked the carpenter. "I have built a magnificent pavilion for the emperor. Here he can sit in the shade and think. This must be the Garden for Noble Thoughts."

"No, no," insisted the bricklayer. "Noble thoughts are fine but first the emperor must be guided to the pavilion before he thinks. Here are my bricks to lead his royal steps. Surely this is the Garden of Guided Steps."

The stonecutter smiled.

"You have all created a garden most worthy of the emperor," he said, "but he will never see any of it until he walks through my beautiful carved gate. Must not this be the Garden Through the Carved Gate?"

Each villager wanted to name the garden for his own work. No two people could agree on a name. Children argued with parents. Neighbor argued with friend.

Soon everyone was yelling at everyone else. The village was still poor but it was no longer agreeable.

The rains were very hard that year. They swelled the river so that it overflowed its banks and flooded the new garden, filling the pond with fish and spreading a thick layer of mud over the melons.

When the rains finally stopped, the villagers went to see their garden.

"Oh, no," they cried. "It is ruined! We must not show this terrible garden to the emperor. We will be shamed."

And so, when the emperor's caravan came into the village, the people lined the streets as usual, with bowed heads, hoping that the emperor would not stop to visit.

But instead of passing silently on, the emperor's horses stopped and the emperor himself stood upon the humble ground of the poor village and spoke in his majestic voice to the schoolteacher.

"I hear that you have made a special garden for me," the emperor said. "I would like to see it."

"O Eternal Being, the monsoons have made the garden unworthy of your sight," the schoolteacher said.

"I will see it all the same," said the emperor.

The shame-faced schoolteacher led the emperor to the garden while the villagers reluctantly followed behind.

The emperor walked through the stone gate, onto the newly washed brick path, and into the little wooden pavilion. He looked out upon the mud-covered melons and opened his mouth to speak. The villagers trembled at what terrible anger the emperor must feel at seeing such a garden.

"What a lovely little hill," the emperor said.

The farmer, who had feared what the emperor might say, looked at his mud-covered melons and saw they did indeed form a very pleasant hill.

The emperor then sat on a bench and was silent for a moment. The carpenter, too, was afraid of what thoughts the emperor must be thinking.

But the emperor smiled and said, "This is a fine place for thinking. And when I am finished thinking, I can turn my eyes to the most delightful sight of fish swimming over the colorful, sparkling stones."

The children, who had been hiding behind their parents, came out to look in surprise at the bright, wet stones on the bottom of the pond.

"And that peach tree," said the emperor, "reminds me of the long and fruitful life I have." The gardener ran to the tree and plucked the ripest peach from its branches. She bowed very low when she presented it to the emperor.

Walking back from the garden, the emperor declared, "This is a most noble garden, but as I walk along this perfect brick path, there is one thing that troubles me."

The villagers held their breath. Had they argued so loudly that the emperor heard them all the way from his palace?

"Please tell us, O Divine Presence, what we have done to displease you," begged the schoolteacher.

"You have not named your garden," the emperor said.

"We would be honored if you would choose its name," said the villagers.

"It is a splendid garden where all things come together in perfect agreement," the emperor said. "I will name it the Garden of Supreme Harmony."

As soon as the emperor left, the villagers set about cleaning the garden. The farmer fertilized the peach tree while the gardener smoothed out the mud on the watermelon hill. The ditchdigger and the bricklayer worked together to sweep the bricks around the pond. The children and their parents gathered bits of food to feed the fish. The carpenter steadied the ladder so that the stonecutter could carve the name of the emperor's garden on the entrance gate.

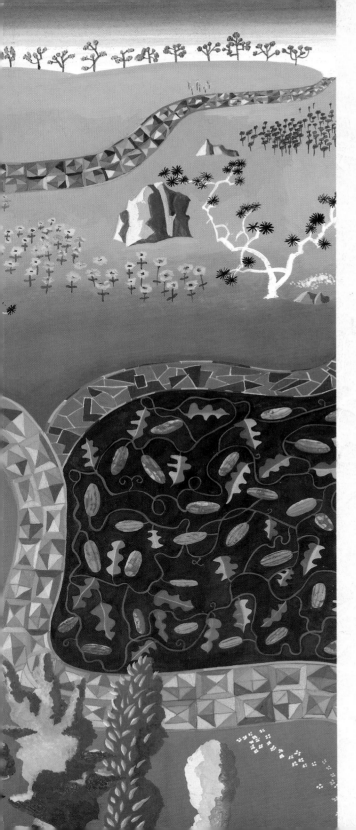

And each year the Emperor and his children and his
children's children would stop in the village on the way
to the Summer Palace. For the Garden of Supreme
Harmony, while not the biggest or the richest or the
fanciest in China, was a most agreeable garden.